I enjoy sl...
my books ...
I do my
friends, as...
only that you tr...
them well and see
them safely home

THE FLINT HILLS FOAL

THE FLINT HILLS FOAL

Dorothy Brenner Francis
illustrated by Taylor Oughton

Abingdon
Nashville

THE FLINT HILLS FOAL

Copyright © 1976 by Abingdon

Library of Congress Cataloging in Publication Data

Francis, Dorothy Brenner.
  The Flint Hills foal.

  SUMMARY: Unhappy since her Father's remarriage, Kathy's
life changes when a valuable foal becomes lost on the prairie
during a storm.
  [1. Horses—Fiction] I. Oughton, Taylor, 1925- II. Title.
PZ7.F8466Fl   [Fic]   76-4812

ISBN 0-687-13189-8

For
Pat
and
Hawkeye Twister

Contents

Chapter One
Thunderhead

Kathy Duncan leaned forward in the saddle as she cantered across the bluestem prairie. The grass gave off a sweet perfume, but Kathy sensed danger in the steaming air that slapped her face. Although a storm was brewing, she was almost beyond caring. Her life had become one big storm ever since Jay King came to live at her house.

Kathy peered into the distance. That Jay! She saw her stepbrother sitting hunched on a knoll about a quarter of a mile away. She knew he was bent over his super-secret sketchbook. He was probably drawing a picture of the very cloud that was about to drench him.

"Come on, Dynamite!" Kathy's thick braids flapped against her shoulders with the motion of her horse. Her damp shirt clung to her back as the sun blazed hotter and hotter. When she reached Jay, she reined the sweat-flecked chestnut to a stop. Jay snapped his sketchbook shut.

"You're supposed to come home," Kathy said. "Flo's orders."

"Mom promised me I could stay all day." Jay patted the grease-stained sack at his side. "She even packed me a lunch."

"She changed her mind." Kathy sighed. "You're supposed to come home. It's going to rain."

Suddenly Kathy almost laughed. Jay was a handsome boy with blue eyes, blonde hair, and a deep suntan. But he had a busy face—like a rabbit's. He was always wrinkling his forehead or twitching his nose. And he was forever chewing bubble gum.

"What's so funny?" Jay asked.

"Nothing." Kathy wiped the grin from her face.

Jay looked to the northwest where a cloud was billowing up. As he stared at it, the cloud covered the sun, leaving patches where light streamed through.

"That's the only cloud in the sky," he

said. "It's pure white. There's no storm coming. You've gotta be kidding."

"You're not in New York now," Kathy said. "Storms blow up fast in these Flint Hills. You're staring right at the start of a Kansas thunderhead." Thunderhead. That was a big word. Kathy hoped Jay would be impressed.

He shrugged. "Who's afraid? I've been in worse storms than you've ever seen. Once I was lost in the mountains for five days. It was snowing all the time. Now that was a storm! But I wasn't scared."

Kathy knew Jay was bragging. Another tall tale. But she didn't yell "horsefeathers." She wanted to please her dad by getting along with Jay.

Along the ground the wind whipped from the south. Kathy watched the top of the cloud flare out from the north; high above the ground the wind was shifting. She sniffed the scent of rain.

"Let's get out of here. Climb on. We'll ride double."

"Nothing doing," Jay said. "You go on. I'll walk."

"You can have the saddle, and I'll ride behind."

"I told you I'd walk," said Jay, scowling.

Kathy glared back at him. She hated Jay King. Some of her friends fussed about their real brothers. Well! She could tell them that a stepbrother was double trouble. Jay loved getting her in bad with her father. Like right now. She wanted to do what her dad and Flo had asked, but she couldn't force Jay to ride.

As they argued, lightning zigzagged electric arrows across the sky. Thunder rumbled a warning. Dynamite whinnied and pranced, every muscle tense.

"We better cut out of here," Kathy said. "Get on."

"No!" Jay shouted and started running toward home.

Kathy trotted Dynamite beside Jay for a while. But as thunder shook the whole prairie, she had a hard time holding the mare back.

"Get on," she shouted once more.

Jay shook his head and kept on running. The air cooled as the wind began blowing in

great gusts. It billowed the bluestem until the prairie looked like a blue-gray ocean. Kathy glanced over her shoulder just as a rolling cloud boiled onto the horizon like black liquid.

Dime-size rain drops pelted Dynamite's hide. She bolted, and Kathy couldn't hold her back. What would Flo and Dad say when she rode in without Jay?

The rain hit like silver needles as Dynamite galloped into the Richfield Ranch where Kathy worked part time. Hank Henry, the stable manager, hobbled to the corral gate.

"I'll take care of Dynamite," he shouted. "You scat for home."

In spite of his limp, Hank had a solid look about him. His hair was silver. He had silver frames on his glasses. And his eyes were a silver gray. He reminded Kathy of pure sterling. She often wished that she had known him before his accident.

"Do you need help?" She yelled above the roar of the storm.

"No!" Hank shouted. "Git for home. Git, I say."

"What about Flash?" Kathy cupped her hands to shield her eyes from the rain. "What about my foal?"

"Flash and her mother are in the box stall." Hank pointed. "Now will you git?"

Kathy ran. She was drenched by the time she reached the back door of the white frame house. Once inside, she was pelted with questions.

"You mean you just left him out there on the prairie?" Flo demanded. "All alone?"

Flo hardly ever looked straight at Kathy. Usually she sort of peeked at her. But now Flo stared at her. And Flo's eyes said that Kathy was to blame for Jay's not being home.

Kathy's tongue felt clumsy as a cinch strap as she tried to explain to her stepmother. "He wouldn't come with me. Then Dynamite bolted, and . . ."

"Rick!" Flo turned to Kathy's father, who was already ramming his arms into a yellow slicker.

"I'll go after him," Rick said. "Now don't worry." He patted Flo's arm and smiled, but when he looked at Kathy his mouth was a

15

straight line. He said nothing, but Kathy wondered what he was thinking. She felt as if a barbed-wire fence had grown up between them ever since Jay had come to Kansas to live.

Chapter Two
Jay King

Kathy watched her dad dart from the house. He was a big man who always walked as if he had springs in his shoes. As he eased into the Volkswagen, he reminded Kathy of a whale squeezing into a sardine can. But Rick Duncan sold Volkswagens, so the family had to drive one.

The Duncan house sat at the edge of town, the city park on one side, and the Richfield Ranch on the other. Kathy's backyard blended into the rolling Flint Hills. She watched the Volkswagen for only a few minutes before it disappeared into the prairie.

"Put on some dry clothes." Flo snapped her fingers. "You're dripping on my carpet."

Kathy felt her face flush. She must look like a soggy monochrome. Monochrome. Kathy liked big words, and she knew what that one meant. Before her dad had married Flo he used to call Kathy his monochrome. She had looked it up. A monochrome was a picture painted in different shades of the same color. Kathy and her father both had dark brown hair, light brown eyes, and tanned skin.

If she and Dad were monochromes, Flo must be a pastel polychrome. Her colors were all light and gay. She was so beautiful that Kathy felt ugly.

She supposed her stepmother had ears, but Kathy had never seen them. Flo's honey-colored hair streamed from a center part to her shoulders. It hung like corn silk against her creamy skin.

But it was her walk that Kathy admired most. She had a gait like a thoroughbred. Her strides were long and easy. She was the kind of person who could jaywalk across a busy street without hurrying.

After she changed into a dry robe and slippers, Kathy felt better. She got out some peanuts and gumdrops she had hidden in her desk drawer. Flo hated for her to hide food in her room, but Kathy did it anyway. Knowing that she had some secret snacks made her feel safe.

She ate one nut and three gumdrops before she joined Flo in the kitchen. They peered out the back window, but it was no use. The rain sheeted against the pane; they could see no farther than the backyard.

The backyard embarrassed Kathy. Flo had made a bathroom in it. Before she married Rick and moved to Kansas, she had been a decorator. And when she had moved into the Duncan house, she insisted that they remodel. The bathroom was first. It suited Kathy just fine; she liked the new pink bathtub and the polished tile floor.

The thing she hated was Flo's idea for using the old bathroom fixtures for yard decorations. Flo thought it would be cute. The sink was now a birdbath. The bathtub was a goldfish pool with lily pads and snails. And the you-know-what served as a planter for petunias and marigolds. It was awful. Kathy never invited her friends over anymore.

"Here they are," Flo called.

Kathy dashed to the door and flung it open. Her dad and Jay and lots of water came in at the same time.

"Are you all right?" Flo took Jay's soaked sketchbook and helped him from his dripping shirt.

"Sure, Mom." Jay spoke through chattering teeth. "It's just a little rain."

Jay seldom complained. That one quality helped make him bearable. Kathy tried to remember it when he got her in trouble. She tried to remember it when he bragged and when he made such a show of keeping his sketchbook private. She tried to like Jay because her dad wanted her to. But it wasn't working out.

Jay didn't like any of the things Kathy did. That evening after he dried out, he wanted to play Monopoly. Jay liked to count money and to add and subtract. Kathy couldn't keep her mind on the game.

"You landed on Park Place!" Jay crowed. "And I have two hotels there. You owe me . . ." He paused to do some figuring.

Kathy shoved all her play money toward

Jay. "Who cares about Monopoly!" She twisted the end of her left braid around her forefinger. "I was thinking about Flash. She's only two weeks old, and this is the first storm she's ever seen. I hope she's not scared."

"Don't see how you can get so worked up about horses." Jay wriggled his nose. "They're smelly, and they draw flies. And . . ."

"Mr. Richfield put me in charge of Flash," Kathy said. "I'm supposed to handle her— get her used to people. Mr. Richfield owns the ranch and the Bluestem Stables, you know. If I do a good job now, he may let me help break her later. I don't want Flash to be frightened by anything."

"I like dogs better than horses." Jay wrinkled his forehead. "In New York I owned five St. Bernards. They all won blue ribbons at the dog shows."

Horsefeathers! Kathy knew Jay had lived in an apartment in New York. An apartment would hardly hold five St. Bernards. But she said nothing. She just disliked him a little more.

The Flint Hills Foal

"Do you really like that dumb job at the stables?" Jay asked. "For no money?"

"I wouldn't do it if I didn't love it. I'm the only fifth grader in my room who has a part-time job. And I get paid. I get to ride whenever I want to, and Hank's teaching me all about horses. That's worth more than money. Besides, it's fun to exercise the horses and help groom them."

"Hank's just working you," Jay said. "With that bum leg of his, he can't handle his job. He's tricking you into doing part of it for him."

"Don't know how I could be so lucky," Kathy said. "Hank knows enough about horses to write a book. He knows what a horse is going to do an instant before the horse does it."

"What's the matter with his leg? Or is that limp just a put-on?"

"When Hank was young he was almost killed in a harness racing accident. His own carelessness caused it. He had to give up riding and racing, but nothing could make him give up horses. Did you know he has seven wooden legs?"

22

"Nobody has seven wooden legs," Jay said.

"Nobody but Hank. They're hanging on the wall in the tack shed at the stable. Hank says he wants them in sight to remind him to be careful."

"Nobody has seven wooden legs," Jay shouted. "You're a liar."

"It takes one to spot one." Kathy shouted and stuck her tongue out—and just at that moment her dad paused in the doorway. She tried to ignore the disappointment in his eyes as she ran to her room and slammed the door shut.

Jay had scored again. He had made her look bad in front of her father. Twice in the same day!

Kathy ate a cracker from a tin that was hidden in her room. She wished she could go to the stables right that minute. The horses loved her, and she loved them. The stables were the only place where she really felt at home.

Kathy finally went to sleep dreaming about wooden legs and St. Bernards. She dreamed that her dad's mouth was just a straight line that someone had painted on his face.

Every time she awakened, Kathy heard the rain splatting against the roof, against the windowpanes. But when morning came, the sun was shining. Kathy bounced from bed and looked at her watch. She wasn't due at the stables for an hour. But as she slipped into jeans and T-shirt, something drew her to the window.

All at once Kathy felt hollow inside. A white truck was leaving the Richfield Ranch. Hank hobbled to close the gate behind it. As the truck turned down the road, Kathy read the words lettered on its side. NATIONAL BY-PRODUCTS INC. And in smaller print, Dead Stock Removed.

Chapter Three
After the Storm

The morning silence told Kathy that her father had gone to work and that Flo was still asleep. Hurrying to the kitchen, she almost ran into Jay.

"Where are you going?" Jay wrinkled his forehead and snapped a pink wad of bubble gum.

"To the stables." Kathy poured some milk in a glass and swallowed it in three gulps.

"It's too early," Jay argued.

Kathy hesitated. "There's been an accident." Slamming the glass down on the counter, she ran out the back door. A lump the size of a currycomb blocked her throat, and she was in no mood to talk to Jay.

"How do you *know*?" Jay called.

Kathy pretended not to hear. She had run clear to the corral before she noticed Jay tagging along behind. Hank hobbled through the mud to meet them, but his easy smile was missing.

Kathy wanted to shout, "What happened? What happened?" but she was afraid of the answer. Instead, she stared at the sign on the corral gate until the white letters blurred into the blue background.

Richfield Ranch & Bluestem Stables
Horses Boarded
&
Trained
A. J. Richfield, Owner

In keeping with the name, the stable buildings were painted bright blue. The barn, the tack shed, even the corral fence— all were blue. Today it seemed the blue of sadness.

"I saw the truck." Kathy said, finding her voice at last.

"It was Mr. Richfield's mare." Hank shook his head. "Storm scared her. She smashed through two gates and jumped a fence. Lightning struck her out in the hills."

"Oh, no!" Kathy cried. She had known Duchess since she was a yearling. Duchess was her favorite of all the horses at the Bluestem.

"Dumb horse," Jay said, twitching his nose.

Kathy scowled at him. She twirled the end of one brown braid around her finger and looked back at Hank. "What about Flash?"

"The foal's disappeared." Hank stared at a spot just above Kathy's head. "I drove the jeep and searched everywhere. No sign of it."

Tears stung Kathy's eyelids. "She must be somewhere near. I'll hunt for her. Don't worry, Hank. I'll find her. Mr. Richfield's counting on me."

Hank shook his head. "Listen, Kathy. I've hunted. If that foal were alive, I'd have found her."

"You were in the jeep. I'll walk. Maybe you were going too fast to see her."

"An orphan foal doesn't have much of a chance." Hank patted Kathy on the shoulder. "Why don't you just stick around the stables today? Blitzen and Dynamite rolled in the mud this morning. Lots of grooming to be done." Hank ran a leathery hand across his silvered hair.

"But the foal," Kathy insisted. "Mr. Richfield's coming home on Friday. What'll he say if Flash isn't here? He's counting on me to take care of her for him."

"What'll he say when he finds his Duchess isn't here either?" Hank asked. "I hate to have to give him that piece of news. But there was nothing anyone could do. And breaking your heart over that foal won't help either."

"I'm going to find Flash." Kathy stiffened her back and stood as tall as she could. "She's gotta be around here someplace."

Hank stepped so close to her that Kathy could smell the mixture of leather and pipe tobacco that clung to his clothes. She thought he was going to forbid her to leave the stables. Instead he just shook his head again and cleared his throat.

"Found the mare off to the north." Hank nodded toward the rolling prairie.

Kathy climbed over the corral fence and headed north. Flash would have followed her mother. Kathy gulped. She wouldn't let herself cry. Flash would be hard enough to find without having to look through tears.

The wet grass soaked her shoes and jeans before she had gone far, but Kathy paid no attention. She had climbed one knoll and was sliding into a V-shaped ravine before Jay caught up with her.

"You're a dope," he said. "Hank told you there's no use looking."

"No one's making you come along." Kathy hoped Jay would take the hint and leave. She knew she could look in spots that no jeep could reach.

"Nothing else to do." Jay hurried to keep up with her. "Why do they call this place the Flint Hills?"

"Because some of the rock under the soil is flint. The Indians used to make their arrowheads from it."

"I don't believe you," Jay said. "Your father says this bluestem grows over a bed of limestone. He says that's why the grass is so full of minerals and so good for cattle."

"Then why'd you ask me?" Kathy

29

scowled. Jay could talk to her father. Why couldn't she talk to him anymore?

She walked faster hoping Jay would tire and turn back. Once when she saw a splash of tan against the bluestem, she ran toward it. But it was just a dried patch of thistle.

Jay stopped talking, but he stayed close beside her. The sun pounding on the damp grass turned the whole prairie into a giant steam table. Kathy explored every nook and niche that could hide a foal. But she saw nothing except bluestem grass and black and white Holsteins grazing in the distance. By mid-morning her legs felt heavy as posts. She sat down to rest, and Jay plopped down beside her.

"Maybe Flash fell into the creek," he said.

Kathy scowled and mopped her forehead on her shirttail. Jay had a way of saying the very things she wanted to push from her mind. The rain had turned the spring-fed stream into a rushing torrent. Kathy knew she had to search it before she returned to the ranch. What if Flash had drowned?

Chapter Four
Search in the Flint Hills

"Is that foal really so special?" Jay asked.

"She's a dun quarter horse," Kathy said, as if that explained everything. "She's registered, and her markings are great."

"What markings?" Jay asked. "I didn't notice anything great about her."

Kathy sighed. How could Jay have looked at Flash and not noticed how perfect she was?

"She has a black mane and tail. She has a single black stripe down her back." Kathy ticked the markings off on her fingers. "She has dark zebra bands on the backside of her legs behind the knees. And besides all that, her right hind leg has a white stocking and there's a white snip on her forehead. Mr. Richfield let me name her. She's going to be a beautiful horse."

"I think she's dead." Jay wriggled his nose. "If she were alive, we would have seen her by now. She must have weighed a hundred pounds."

"Hank said she weighed about that much when she was born." Kathy fanned herself with her shirttail. "And she's two weeks old now."

"She's dead," Jay repeated. "There's nothing alive around here that weighs over a hundred pounds."

"Quit saying that," Kathy snapped. "She might be hurt. She might be lying anywhere around here. This grass is so tall in places that it's hard to see anything on the ground until you're right on it."

"I hate Kansas," Jay said. "There's nothing here but grass and cows and more grass and more cows. And this heat! I'll be glad when next month comes. I get to visit my dad in July. He has custody, too, you know. Mom and Dad had a big fight over who got to keep me."

Custody. Kathy knew what that word meant, too. And she hated it. Her parents hadn't fought over who got custody of her.

When her mom left, the judge gave custody to her dad.

Kathy guessed that he hadn't really wanted custody. Anyway, he never smiled at her very much anymore. And he was always scolding her about sitting on Flo's new furniture with her horsey clothes. But he had plenty of smiles for Flo. And for Jay.

Kathy dug into her pocket for the raisins she had hidden there. She offered one to Jay to be polite and was glad when he refused it.

"There were big headlines in the papers about it," he said.

"About what?" Kathy asked.

"About who got custody. Dad put up a battle, but Mom won. I have to live here eleven months of the year. Eleven months! I tried to talk to the judge, but he wouldn't listen."

Horsefeathers. Kathy said the word in her mind. That's what Jay's big talk was—just a bunch of horsefeathers. There probably hadn't been anything in the papers at all. It was just another of Jay's tall tales like the one about the five St. Bernards or the one about the snowstorm that lasted for five days.

Kathy knew kids who bragged about how badly their parents wanted custody of them. And she knew that all that bragging was just a cover-up for a fear like her own—fear that no one really wanted custody. Custody. She hated the word.

"I saw Hank's seven wooden legs," Jay said, changing the subject.

"Did he show them to you?" Kathy felt a stab of jealousy.

"Naw. I peeked through the tack shed window. Guess I shouldn't have called you a liar."

Kathy scowled. Why wasn't her dad ever around to hear the good things that were said?

"What's he need so many for?" Jay asked.

"Those are old legs that he's worn out. He says they remind him to be careful."

"They give me the creeps," said Jay, shuddering.

"They remind him that a person can never be absolutely sure of what any horse is going to do." Kathy stood up and headed toward the stream, dreading what she might find there. Jay followed, and for once she was glad. She really hated being alone. And for once Jay did seem to be trying to help.

The stream was like a silver magnet that pulled them across the prairie, into rain-washed gullies, into heat-filled ravines. But there was no sign of Flash.

"Dumb foal." Jay popped his bubble gum. "Any animal with half a brain would have stayed in its stall. I don't like horses."

"Flash followed her mother." Kathy's voice shrilled at Jay's unfair words.

"Dumb mare," Jay said. "You'd think a grown animal would be smarter than that. I thought horses were intelligent."

"It's the nature of grazing animals to run when they're afraid," Kathy said. "Hank told me that. Lions and tigers have fangs and claws for protection. A horse only has its legs. So it runs."

"I'm going home," Jay said. "It's almost lunchtime. Maybe my sketchbook's dried out by now."

"Tell Flo I won't be there for lunch," Kathy said.

"Aren't you hungry?"

Kathy shook her head. She had lost all appetite the moment she had seen the white truck leaving the Richfield Ranch.

After Jay left, Kathy tramped on, following the swollen stream. Her feet grew heavy as bricks. Her mouth was parched. As the sun dropped toward the horizon, she knew she must have walked for miles. She was resting when she saw Hank's blue jeep bouncing toward her.

"Any luck?" Hank stopped beside Kathy and motioned for her to get in.

She shook her head. "But I haven't given up. Flash has to be around here somewhere. A foal just can't disappear."

"Well, you've had enough for one day," Hank said. "Climb in."

As Kathy got in, she knew for sure that Hank agreed with Jay. His face said so. They both thought Flash was dead. So! They were both wrong. They had to be. Kathy knew Flash was alive. Tomorrow she would find her—tomorrow when she was rested. She wondered how long a foal could live without food, but she was afraid to ask.

Chapter Five
Search to the South

Kathy ate her supper that night. It tasted like straw, but it was easier to eat than explain why she wasn't hungry. From the corner of her eye she saw Flo peeking at her, but her stepmother said nothing.

"I heard about the bad luck at the stables last night," Kathy's dad said. "Too bad. Mr. Richfield lost a valuable mare."

Grown-ups! Kathy stared at her plate. Grown-ups were only sorry because the mare was worth a lot of money. They didn't care that she was the most beautiful quarter horse in Kansas. They didn't care that she had been one of the best cow horses in the Flint Hills. They didn't care that she had been Kathy's friend.

"The foal's still missing." Jay grabbed his

37

chance to get his stepfather's attention. "It's sure to be dead by now."

Kathy glared at him. He didn't sound one bit sorry.

"I do wish you'd change into clean clothes before you come to the table." Flo peeked at Kathy, then smiled at Rick, expecting him to agree.

Mr. Duncan cleared his throat. Kathy clamped her jaws together and braced herself for a scolding.

"Kathy, when you go onto the prairie tomorrow, take a lunch with you. Promise?"

Kathy looked up, surprised. Her dad wasn't smiling, but there was concern in his eyes. He said nothing about her clothes. And he had said "when you go," not "if you go." Surely he must think there was a chance that Flash was alive. Sometimes what her dad didn't say was more important than what he did say.

"Okay, Dad," Kathy replied. "I'm going to hunt for Flash as long as there's any chance she might be alive."

Kathy slipped three red grapes into her pocket while Flo wasn't looking. As soon as she had helped clear the supper dishes, she ducked into her room. She was in no mood for Monopoly. She was in no mood for Jay and his bragging and his secret sketchbook.

Once alone, Kathy hid the three grapes inside the black china stallion that stood on her bookcase. She checked her supply of peanuts and crackers. Flo hadn't found them yet.

Kathy was so tired she went right to bed, but the next morning she was up at sunrise. She was halfway out the back door when she remembered about the lunch. Tip-toeing back to the kitchen, she made a sandwich. She stuffed it and an apple into a brown sack and headed toward the prairie.

Although Hank had found the mare north of the stables, today Kathy headed south. She had searched the north area thoroughly the day before.

Dew glazed the bluestem. The grass swished against her ankles like a tangle of wet strings.

Kathy usually loved the fresh, clean smell of the prairie, but today she hardly noticed. She was intent on her search. She didn't duck when honey bees zoomed by her ears. She didn't jump when grasshoppers landed right on her bare arms. She tramped from one gulley to the next. She climbed from one knoll to another. Then she followed the winding stream which had eased back into its banks. Kathy lost all track of time, but the sun was blazing high overhead before she stopped to rest.

"Any luck?"

Kathy jumped as Jay surprised her from behind. Before she could answer, he went on talking.

"What you need is a helicopter. You could fly over this whole area and see everything here in about five minutes."

"Sure," Kathy said. "Any other good ideas?"

Jay flopped down and opened his sketchbook to a fresh page.

"How dare you sit around drawing pictures at a time like this."

"If I thought Flash was alive, I'd help you hunt. But I'm not wasting my time on a dead foal."

Kathy was about to tell Jay off when

something overhead caught her eye. She jumped to her feet. But when she tried to speak, her tongue would hardly work.

"I know where Flash is." Kathy's voice sounded so low and shivery she almost scared herself. Even Jay's blue eyes grew round as horseshoes.

"Look!" Kathy whispered, pointing toward their left where three large birds etched black circles against the sky.

"Buzzards!" Jay's mouth fell open. "I've seen 'em on TV. Look at those bald heads! Those fellows don't move in until an animal's dead. I told you it was too late."

"They haven't moved in yet," Kathy said. "They're still circling."

She dashed toward the area the huge birds seemed to be guarding. Then she stopped, afraid of what she would see.

Swallowing her fear, she eased down a gentle slope into a sun-baked ravine. The eerie birds swooped lower and lower. It was a few moments before Kathy saw Flash's still form sprawled behind a small outcropping of limestone.

Chapter Six
Wanted: One Miracle

Kathy tiptoed toward Flash. Was she dead? Her eyes were open, but they were unseeing as glassy brown marbles. Flies swarmed around her head. Her coat was matted and muddy. Several seconds passed before Kathy was sure Flash was breathing. Inching closer, she knelt beside her.

"Flash." Kathy whispered, shooing the flies. "Flash!" She spoke louder and rubbed the foal's neck and withers. Flash blinked and pricked one ear forward. Kathy wanted to throw her arms around the foal. She wanted to burst into tears of joy, but Jay was at her side. She could only feel the matted roughness of Flash's coat beneath her fingers.

"Creepers!" Jay whispered. "She is alive. What're you going to do now?"

"I'm staying right here while you go get Hank. Tell him to call the vet and bring the truck."

"You're going to stay here alone?" Jay eyed the three buzzards that still circled overhead.

"Of course," Kathy said. "I can't leave Flash. Get going, will you?"

For once Jay didn't argue or scoff or brag. He took off running.

Kathy talked to Flash. She stroked her ears. She patted her nose.

Suddenly she noticed the foal felt very hot. Flash needed a drink. Kathy glanced around. What could she carry water in? She kicked off her shoes and skinned from her socks. After pulling her shoes back on, she jogged to the stream. It took precious moments to rinse the socks out. As soon as they were clean, Kathy carried them dripping back to where Flash lay.

Now what? Flash was too weak to lift her head. Kathy rubbed a wet sock over the foal's nose. Then she eased her thumb into the side of Flash's mouth and pried her jaws open. Kathy managed to squeeze a few drops of water onto the foal's tongue. She would have squeezed more, but she was afraid of choking her.

It seemed as if a calendar of Sundays had passed before Kathy heard the rumble of the truck. As it bounced closer, she saw three people in the cab—Hank, Jay, and Dr. Pillum. Hank had waited for the veterinarian. That's what had taken so long.

As Hank stopped the truck, Dr. Pillum stepped out and walked toward Kathy. She wanted to shout to him to hurry. She watched the sun glint on the fringe of hair that circled his bald head like a halo of steel wool. Something in the no-hurry way he moved comforted her. It was as if his whole body were saying, "Now keep calm. Everything's going to be all right."

But that was not what Dr. Pillum said after he examined Flash.

"She's in a bad way, Hank." He straightened up and shook his head. "Has a high temperature. Not much chance of saving her, but I'll give her an antibiotic."

Antibiotic. A chemical that would destroy germs. Kathy concentrated on the big word.

Maybe if she thought only about it she could forget the rest of Dr. Pillum's ominous statement.

After easing Flash onto a blanket sling, the men lifted her into the truck bed. Dr. Pillum gave the foal a shot. Flash didn't even wince at the prick of the needle.

"You kids ride in back with Flash," Hank said. "We'll do all we can for her."

Kathy climbed into the truck bed, but Jay hung back. "I'd rather ride in the cab."

Dr. Pillum shrugged. "Be my guest."

Even though Hank drove slowly in low gear, the truck still bounced on the rough prairie. Kathy held one hand under Flash's head to cushion the jolts. She talked to her all the way to the stable. Kathy was glad Jay had ridden with the men. He would have laughed at her for talking to a horse.

Dr. Pillum and Hank bedded Flash in an airy stall, then Dr. Pillum spoke. "I'll check on her again this evening, Hank, but there's not much we can do."

"What about feeding her?" Kathy asked. "She'll die without some food. I could try to get her to drink from a bottle."

"It won't hurt to try," Dr. Pillum said. "But don't get your hopes up. It's hard to bottle feed a healthy foal, let alone one that's more dead than alive." He reached into his bag of supplies.

"Here Fit this rubber nipple onto a pop bottle. Mix a quart of skimmed cow's milk with one tablespoon of white syrup. Better add a little egg white too. Heat it until it's just warm to the touch. You may have to dilute the whole mixture with some water so it won't taste so strange to her. But I doubt if she'll take it no matter what you do or how you fix it."

"You t-think she's going to d-die, don't you?" Kathy couldn't control the waver in her voice.

"Now, Kathy." Dr. Pillum smiled. "I didn't say that. Every doctor believes in miracles. And that's what it'll take to save this foal."

Chapter Seven
Formula for Flash

Kathy felt Hank's gaze as she watched Dr. Pillum leave the ranch. "I'll get Flash to eat, Hank," she said, facing him. "Flash knows me. And horses remember. She'll eat for me."

"Now, don't you go a-getting your hopes blown up like a balloon," Hank warned. "That foal's almost done for."

"I'll try to feed her as long as she's alive," Kathy insisted. "How much milk do you think it will take?"

"Probably none." Hank sighed and tapped his pipe against his wooden leg. "But if she should start eating, you can count on her taking a good two gallons a day."

"Two gallons!" Kathy blurted. "That's almost as much milk as Flo buys in a week."

"I don't doubt it," said Hank. "And milk's not free."

"I've got some money," Kathy said. "That I've been saving to buy a horse of my own."

"I'll advance you whatever you need," Hank said. "Mr. Richfield would want me to."

"I'll lend you money if you run out," Jay offered. "You'll have to pay me back, though. And with interest."

Kathy said, "I'll use my own money. I want to do something for Flash. But let's not argue about that now. I've got to mix a bottle of milk formula right away. Flash hasn't eaten for a day and a half." Formula. Formula. Kathy liked the important sound of that word. And she didn't need to look it up. She was sure that in this case it was another word for miracle.

Although Kathy hated to leave Flash for even an instant, she sprinted home. Jogging through the garage, she grabbed a six-pack of empty cola bottles as she whizzed by them.

"Flo never uses skim milk," Kathy said, as they ran into the kitchen.

48

"Then we'll have to buy some," Jay said.

Kathy dashed to her room and shook coins from her bank. One minute Jay was getting her in big trouble with her father. And the next minute he was acting like her best friend. She couldn't figure him out. But she didn't trust him. Not one bit. A boy who disliked horses could never rate with her.

Jay walked with Kathy to the corner grocery. Maples and oaks arched overhead like a green leafy tunnel. But the cement sidewalk caught the midday heat and threw it back into their faces.

Kathy welcomed the coolness of the grocery store. Inhaling the odor of melons and bananas, she followed Jay to the dairy case. He picked up a quart of milk.

"That's not enough. Hank said two gallons."

"If the foal starts eating," Jay reminded. "A quart should be enough for now."

"I'm taking no chances," Kathy said firmly. "I've got enough money for two gallons, and that's what I'm going to buy."

After she paid for the milk, they plodded

home. Kathy was glad Jay had come. She could never have carried all four half-gallon cartons by herself.

When they got home, Kathy sat down at the kitchen table with pencil and paper. She had always been slow at arithmetic, and now was no time for mistakes. She figured carefully for a long time; then Jay spoke up.

"It's going to take twenty-two pop bottles if you use the twelve-ounce size."

"How do you know?" Kathy covered her numbers with one hand.

"I figured it up in my head," Jay said. "And there's not that much room in the refrigerator."

Kathy finished multiplying and dividing. She was amazed to find that Jay's answer matched hers. She examined the refrigerator as if she had never seen it before. Two pitchers of pink punch almost filled the top shelf. Three covered pans took up all the space on the second shelf. And there wasn't nearly enough room on the third and fourth shelves for pop bottles to stand upright.

"Guess we're going to have to mix just part of the formula at a time," Kathy said.

"Maybe a half gallon." She figured again.

"That'll only take five or six bottles," Jay said before she could work out the problem on paper.

Kathy found the biggest cooking pan in the cupboard and poured one carton of milk into it. As she reached for the white syrup, Jay said, "I can't get these other three cartons in the refrigerator. There's just no room."

Kathy measured the syrup into the milk before she looked. Jay was right. The milk cartons wouldn't fit.

"Let's take that punch out," he suggested.

Kathy was on guard. Jay was trying to get her into trouble again. "Flo'll have a fit," she said. "We can't do that."

"What else can we do? Milk will sour in this heat, but punch won't. We can stick it back in after Flash drinks some of the formula."

Kathy was persuaded. She was willing to get into trouble if it would help Flash. Removing the punch, she set the milk cartons in its place.

"Dr. Pillum said egg white," Kathy mut-

51

tered. "But how much?"

"He was talking about a quart of milk," Jay reminded. "Maybe he meant one white to each quart—you know, like the syrup."

Kathy took two eggs from the refrigerator. As she stood wondering how to separate the egg yolk from the white, Jay seemed to read her mind. He popped his bubble gum, then spoke.

"First you crack the egg. Then you hold the yellow part in half of the shell while the white drips into a dish."

Kathy set a saucer by the sink, acting as if separating eggs were no special problem. She rapped the egg shell on the counter top. Ugh! Before she could say "horsefeathers," the egg squashed and dripped onto Flo's new kitchen carpet.

Chapter Eight
Kathy Duncan, Nurse

Cleaning egg off a carpet wasn't easy, but Kathy managed. Jay grinned, but he said nothing.

Kathy's fingers felt sticky from syrup and raw egg, but she tried again. This time she tapped the egg gently, the white dripping into the saucer while the yoke remained in one half of the shell. She stirred the egg white into the milk and syrup, then heated the mixture and poured it into the pop bottles. She only spilled a little. She had one more bottle to set in the refrigerator when Flo arrived.

"What on earth are you two doing?" Flo strolled into the room with her long thoroughbred strides. "I'm having a bridge party this afternoon. My guests are due any minute, and this kitchen's a mess."

Flo's sleek pants suit made Kathy pain-
fully aware of her own egg-splattered
cutoffs.

"We're fixing formula for Flash." Kathy
told Flo about the orphan foal. "I'm going to
the ranch right now to try to feed her."

"Kathy, you'll have to take all that milk
with you," Flo said. "Maybe Hank has a
place for it. The punch is for the bridge
party, and it has to be cold. The girls will be
parched on a day like this."

Kathy bit her lower lip to keep it steady as
she removed the milk from the refrigerator.
Jay didn't say a word, and he wouldn't look
at her. She wished her dad were here. He
would tell Flo that formula for an orphan
foal was more important than party punch.
Or would he? Flo had a way with her father
that Kathy didn't understand.

"I know," she said. "I'll use our camping
cooler. I'll fill it with ice and keep Flash's
milk in it until after the party."

"You'll have to run to the store and buy a
bag of ice," Flo said. "I'll need all that's
here. It's over a hundred degrees outside
today."

Flash was starving—maybe dying—and Flo was worrying about a party. How could she!

Flo's blonde hair fell across her face as she dug into her purse. "Here's fifty cents, Kathy. The ice machine is in the parking lot behind the store. Jay, you help carry."

Once outside, Kathy sprinted down the sidewalk. Sweat trickled behind her ears and down the backs of her legs. She was halfway to the store before Jay caught up with her.

"Grown-ups just don't understand." Jay panted the words as they jogged along the sidewalk. "Mom doesn't intend to be mean. She just doesn't understand."

"It's all right." Suddenly Kathy felt sorry for Jay. She never had to apologize for her dad.

It wasn't easy to carry twenty-five pounds of ice back to the house. She and Jay were both hot and sweaty and cross. At first they took turns lugging the bag. The coolness felt good against Kathy's chest, but the bag was heavy and hard to carry. After a few steps they tried sharing the load. Kathy carried one end and Jay the other. That didn't work well either, but that's what they had to do.

By the time they got to the house the bag was dripping like a faucet. Kathy felt icy water trickling from her knee to her ankle, but it didn't cool her off much. When they dumped the ice into the cooler, they saw that almost half of it had melted. But the milk was safe. That was the important thing.

Kathy heated one of the bottles. Just as the party guests began to arrive, she and Jay dashed out the kitchen door and headed toward the stables. Hank was expecting them. He stood by the gate mopping his streaming face with a red bandana. The corral was a pool of heat.

"Jay, you and I'll wait in the tack shed," Hank said. "Flash's used to Kathy. She'll be more apt to eat if we leave them alone."

Jay didn't even look disappointed as he followed Hank. But Kathy didn't care. So what if Jay King didn't like horses? So what!

Kathy smelled the clean odor of fresh straw and fly spray as she eased into Flash's stall. The foal lay like a limp rag. Her coat

was still matted and muddy. Her mane and tail bristled with burrs. She opened her eyes when Kathy spoke her name. Easing the nipple into the foal's mouth, Kathy jiggled it a bit.

"Drink, Flash, drink."

Kathy waited, but Flash closed her eyes. She lay there making no attempt to suck on the nipple. Kathy jiggled it again, squirting a bit of the formula onto Flash's tongue. She didn't open her eyes, but she swallowed.

Kathy wanted to shout the news. Her hands shook, but she kept squirting milk onto Flash's tongue. And Flash kept swallowing—for a while. But soon, she quit drinking. Streams of milk dribbled from the sides of her mouth and dampened the straw under her head. One of the stable cats crept close and tried to lap up the spills.

"Come on, girl," Kathy urged. "Drink. Drink."

But Flash lay there exhausted. Kathy studied the pop bottle. More than two thirds of the formula remained. Tears stung her eyes as she trudged toward the tack shed where Hank and Jay waited.

Chapter Nine
Between Life and Death

Kathy pretended to be interested in her other chores at the ranch. She exercised Blitzen and Dynamite. She groomed them while Jay chewed his gum and drew secret pictures in his sketchbook. Every hour Kathy heated milk for Flash and tried to get her to drink. Hank just watched and shook his head.

When Dr. Pillum arrived at suppertime, Kathy had to tell him the bad news.

"Flash has taken only a bottle and a half of formula all afternoon," Kathy said. "And part of that dribbled on the ground."

"Why, that's better news than I expected," said Dr. Pillum as he walked to Flash's stall. "You've done a good job, Kathy. I'll give her another shot of antibiotic and some vitamins. We'll see how she's doing in the morning."

After he gave the shots, Dr. Pillum and Hank sat down to visit. Kathy and Jay went home for supper.

Afterward Kathy hid a banana behind the horse books in her bookcase. She checked her other hiding places. Everything was okay. Maybe Flo didn't care anymore if she kept a few snacks handy.

It was still broad daylight at eight o'clock when Kathy began heating another bottle of milk. Outside the locusts were buzzing like chain saws, and crickets were beginning to chirp.

"You've been at those stables all day," Flo said, peeking at Kathy from behind her fall of blonde hair. "Surely you're not going back tonight."

"Someone has to feed Flash. And she's used to me. She's just a baby, and she needs to eat often."

"Let her go, Flo," Kathy's father spoke up. "There're worse things a girl her age could be doing. How's Flash coming along, Kathy?" Mr. Duncan's springy footsteps shook the kitchen floor and made the pop bottles rattle.

Kathy felt a warm glow inside. Her father was interested. He had asked! "She only ate a little. But Dr. Pillum said that was good. He's giving her medicine and vitamins."

"Coming, Jay?" Kathy invited him more because her dad was listening than because she wanted his company. But she needn't have worried. Jay wasn't interested.

"You going over there in the dark?" he asked.

It wasn't dark. Kathy sensed that Jay was up to his old trick of trying to get her in trouble. Why couldn't he keep his mouth shut?

"It won't be dark for a long time," she said.

"You be back home before it is," Flo warned.

"Yes, Kathy." Her father agreed with Flo this time. "We don't want to have to come hunting for you." He left the kitchen and eased his huge frame into a chair near the TV.

Kathy said nothing. Sometimes her father

61

was a lot like Jay. One minute he would be on her side, the next minute he would be against her. She didn't understand either of them.

The sun was a brassy disk balanced on a black line of horizon as Kathy jogged to the stables. Hank paused in his early evening chores to wave at her. During the scorching summer months he managed to do his work in the early morning or in the cool of the evening.

Slipping into Flash's stall, Kathy grinned. Flash lifted her head and pricked her ears forward. Kneeling beside the foal, Kathy patted her neck and withers.

"Good girl, Flash," she crooned. "You're feeling better. I can tell."

Flash swished her tail feebly as Kathy offered her the bottle. This time Flash drank over half the formula before she stopped. Kathy brushed one side of the foal's coat with the dandy brush. Gently she removed the burrs from her mane and tail.

"How's it going?" Hank's shadow fell across the foal as he stood in the doorway to the stall.

Kathy held up the bottle of leftover milk. "A little better. She drank over half."

"You're a good nurse," Hank said. "I honestly thought Flash would be dead before night."

Night! Jumping up, Kathy glanced across the prairie. Purple shadows blended into the gray-black sky.

"I've got to go," she said. "Flo and Dad want me home before dark. What am I going to do? Flash should have milk all through the night."

Hank shook his head. "I'll try to get her to take some at ten o'clock before I go to bed. But I can't be up and down like a jack-in-the-box all night long. Doctor has me on sleeping pills. Don't hear much once I get to sleep."

"If you'll feed her at ten, I'll come back at dawn," Kathy said. "I guess that's the best we can do."

Kathy raced home. She took a bath and told everyone goodnight before Jay could suggest a game of Monopoly. She needed to go to bed early if she planned to get up at dawn. Once in her room, Kathy closed the door. She munched on one of the crackers she had hidden under her pillow.

What if Flash got hungry in the night? What if Hank couldn't get her to eat at ten o'clock? What if! What if! Kathy knew she couldn't sleep while Flash was still hovering between life and death.

She set her alarm clock to ring at midnight. If someone didn't feed that foal every few hours, she might die before morning. And Mr. Richfield was counting on Kathy Duncan. Shoving the clock under her pillow where the sound would be muffled, Kathy curled up in a ball and tried to sleep.

Chapter Ten
Midnight Outing

At first Kathy thought the ringing in her ear was the school bell. Then she remembered. The alarm clock. Flash. Groping under her pillow she punched the shut-off button. She held her breath and listened. What if Flo and Dad had heard? Or Jay? The house was silent.

Kathy crept from bed. In the quiet dark she slipped into her clothes. Tiptoeing to the kitchen she opened the refrigerator and took out a bottle of milk. It was hard to heat formula without making any noise, but she managed. Almost.

"What are you doing?" Jay's whisper hit Kathy's eardrums like a knife. She jumped and almost dropped the milk. In the scant light from the stove Jay looked like a ghost.

"I'm going to feed Flash," Kathy whispered. "Go back to bed."

"What if Mom or Rick wake up?" Jay asked.

"If you tell on me, I'll . . . I'll . . ." Kathy hesitated, knowing there was nothing she could do about it if Jay chose to tattle. "Keep quiet, and I'll let you come along." Kathy could almost feel Jay shudder at her suggestion.

"Not me," he whispered. "You go ahead. I'll stuff your pillow under your sheet so it will look as if you're still in bed."

Kathy unlocked the back door and slipped into the night. That Jay! Was he for her or against her? Would he call Flo the minute she was out of sight? She wished Jay had never come to Kansas. Why couldn't he have lived with his father!

Kathy had never been outside alone at midnight. She smelled the earthy dankness of the air. The darkness hung thick and black, yet scary gray shadows leaped and danced across her path. Her scalp felt tight, as if she were wearing a swimming cap.

In the backyard Kathy stumbled over the

bathtub. She dropped the milk bottle right in with the gold fish and the lily pads and the snails. The sleeves of her shirt were wet by the time she had fished it out. Flo and her decorations! Shivering, Kathy eased across the endless space between her backyard and the stables.

Dynamite whinnied as she stepped into the corral, but everything else was quiet. Inside the stable Kathy inhaled the odor of hay and straw and horses. She crept to Flash's stall. It was so dark she had to feel her way. She almost screamed when something brushed against her ankle. Then she realized it was one of the stable cats Hank kept to catch mice.

"Flash!" Kathy whispered the word. Then she spoke softly. "Flash. Time to eat." Groping her way, Kathy touched Flash's mane. The foal snorted and lifted her head. Kathy felt for Flash's mouth and poked the nipple in. She knew by the movements of the bottle in her hand that she was drinking. The foal made little sucking noises. Then suddenly there was a loud slurping sound. Kathy gasped when she realized what it

meant—Flash had finished all the milk. And she was sucking for more.

She knew what she had to do. Outside Flash's stall, Kathy could see better. She ran home through the darkness and heated another bottle of formula. The small light on the stove made an eerie glow in the kitchen. But no one noticed. Not even Jay.

This time Kathy took a flashlight. She was careful when she crept through the backyard. Cutting a wide circle around the bathtub, she made it to the stables with no trouble.

Speaking softly to Flash, she offered the fresh bottle. Flash finished it and stretched out to sleep. Kathy lay down on the soft straw beside her to rest and think for a minute.

For the first time since she had found Flash, Kathy breathed easily. Hank and Dr. Pillum might laugh, but she knew in this moment that Flash was going to live. She was stronger; everyone would be surprised when they saw her in the morning.

Kathy began to worry about taking care of Flash. Could she do it alone? How long would Flo put up with all that formula mixing in her kitchen? Maybe Hank would let her use the tiny kitchen in his quarters.

Kathy wondered what Mr. Richfield would say when he returned on Friday. He was a busy insurance executive; the Blue-stem Stables was only a hobby with him. He wouldn't have time to bottle feed a foal. And Hank already had more than he could do.

Maybe Mr. Richfield would sell Flash to her. She had always wanted a horse of her own. If she owned Flash, her dad would help out whenever she needed him.

Or would he? A nagging doubt played at the back of her mind. He was a lot busier now than he had been before Flo and Jay joined them.

"But what would I use for money, Flash?" Kathy spoke half aloud to the foal. "Maybe if Mr. Richfield doesn't want too much, I could earn you by working for him."

She closed her eyes thinking of having Flash for her very own. Flash nuzzled Kathy's forehead with her moist, velvety nose. She opened her eyes. Daylight! She had fallen asleep!

Kathy leaped up and brushed the straw from her clothes. Outside a white mist hung over the prairie. The sun was a round red broach pinned to the eastern sky.

What would Flo say? Would she forbid her to go back to the stables? What would her Dad do when he found out his daughter had been away all night? Would he make her give up her job helping Hank?

Chapter Eleven
Competition

Kathy ran home, but she braked to a stop at the back door. Holding her breath, she tiptoed inside. Silence. Everyone was still asleep—everyone except Jay. Suddenly Kathy was more frightened than she had been while prowling outside at midnight. No one had missed her. Anything could have happened.

"What's the matter?" Jay asked. "You look sick."

Kathy gulped. No words could explain what it was like not to be missed.

"I fell asleep in Flash's stall," Kathy whispered. "I thought someone might be hunting for me."

"Naw," Jay said. "No one's up yet."

"But I was gone all night," Kathy said.

"So?" Jay laughed and wrinkled his

forehead. "I've been out all night lots of times. Once I was lost in Times Square. Anyway, Mom thought I was lost. I was just out seeing the town, but she called the police. There was a big thing in the paper about it. The police thought I had been kidnapped by five thugs who hung out there. I wasn't scared at all. I was having a ball."

"Oh, horsefeathers!" Kathy said in disgust.

"What's going on out here?" Flo asked, tying the sash on her satin robe as she stepped into the kitchen. "Do you two know it's only five o'clock?"

"We're getting ready to heat milk for the foal," Jay said.

Kathy blinked. Jay was a mystery. He had just passed by a chance to get her into really big trouble. She said nothing, but just began mixing more formula. Flash had drunk all she had prepared yesterday, but she couldn't tell that. Flo might guess that she had been our during the night.

"Well, be quiet," Flo warned. "Rick needs his sleep."

"Thanks, Jay," Kathy said when Flo left the room.

He shrugged his shoulders. "I know how to handle Mom. With both parents wanting custody, a guy learns a lot. Now with my dad it's a different matter. He's not so easy to fool."

More horsefeathers! Kathy turned off her ears. When Jay started talking about custody, she was through listening. She mixed enough formula to last the morning. While it was heating, she washed out the used bottles and prepared to refill them.

Jay walked with her to the stables. After one peek at Flash, he sat down, leaned against the corral fence and began to draw in his secret sketchbook. How could he! Kathy could hardly cork her excitement. Flash was on her feet! She would have shouted the news, but she knew Hank was still asleep.

Now that the foal was up, she seemed to be starving. She slurped the first bottle of milk in a few quick gulps. Kathy was bursting to tell someone. But when she walked toward Jay to show him the empty bottle, he snapped his sketchbook shut and sat on it. Kathy felt her face flush. As if she were interested in Jay's dumb pictures! She promised herself to have no more to do with him. Flash was her only friend—besides Hank, of course.

Kathy ran back to Flash's stall. She could hardly believe the change that had taken place. The foal was bright-eyed and alert. She walked around in her stall and nuzzled Kathy's hand with her soft nose. Although she flopped down often to rest, no one would have guessed that she had been so near death a few short hours ago.

At mid-morning when Dr. Pillum arrived to check on Flash, he was surprised and pleased. "A miracle," he said, smiling at Kathy. "Nothing less than a miracle. Certainly never thought I'd see that foal on her feet again."

After giving Flash another shot, he walked to the tack shed where Hank was standing.

"What do you think Richfield will do with this foal?" Dr. Pillum asked Hank. "He's not going to want to fool around with bottle feeding. And she'll soon be too big for Kathy to handle."

Kathy patted Flash's head and with growing fear listened to the men talk.

"Don't know," Hank said, hobbling to Flash's stall. "Mr. Richfield had big plans for this foal. She's already registered, and I know he planned to show her in halter class just as soon as she was old enough."

"I can feed her." Kathy spoke up for herself. "I'll bottle feed her until she's old enough to eat grain and hay. I want to do it."

"I know you want to, Kathy," Dr. Pillum said. "But you just can't imagine what a job it's going to be. That foal's going to grow. She already outweighs you by thirty or forty pounds. Feeding her's going to be a man's job."

"Afraid I can't handle it," Hank admitted. "I'm just not steady enough on my feet with this bum leg. A foal's naturally playful. Flash could knock me down before I could stop her."

"I have a brother who lives near Emporia." Dr. Pillum polished his belt buckle with his shirt sleeve. "He's retired. Has all the time in the world. I've half a notion to make Mr. Richfield an offer on the foal. My brother could take care of her until she's old enough for me to give to my grandchildren. Those kids would love to have a horse."

Kathy felt as if something inside her had curled up and died. In her imagination Flash was already her foal. They belonged together. They were friends. Since Jay had horned in between her and her dad, Flash was all she had.

Of course Mr. Richfield wouldn't have time to bottle feed a foal. And if he wanted to sell Flash, he would sell to the person with cash. Dr. Pillum. All Kathy could offer was five dollars and her time working at the stables.

"Hank!" Kathy cried after Dr. Pillum got into his car. "Don't let Mr. Richfield sell Flash. You won't let him, will you?"

"Now don't you go fretting," Hank said. "I just don't rightly believe that Mr. Richfield will sell that Flash to anyone."

"Not even to me?" Kathy asked.

"Not to anyone," Hank said. "He's set

great store by that foal. Hauled the mare clear to Kansas City to have her bred. Paid a big fee to get Jayhawk Twister for a sire. No siree! He's not going to sell Flash just because she has to be bottlefed."

Kathy knew Hank meant to make her feel better. But he didn't. She couldn't help thinking of Flash as her own horse. Dr. Pillum was a threat to her dream. He had money, and people with money usually got what they wanted.

Chapter Twelve
One Sore Thumb

Now that Flash was on her feet, Kathy groomed her from head to tail. Her coat was dull and dry as burlap, but Kathy knew it would grow sleek and shiny as Flash grew stronger. She removed the rest of the burrs from her mane and tail. Even though she knew it was too early, still she placed a bit of grain and hay in Flash's feed rack. Even Hank couldn't guess just when a foal might start nibbling solid food.

After the mid-morning feeding Kathy walked over to Jay. She hated to ask him for favors, but she would do almost anything for Flash.

"How about going to the store with me? I'm out of milk."

Jay nodded. He slipped his sketchbook under his shirt, and they went home for money. In her room Kathy counted all the coins in her piggy bank. There was less than five dollars now. With Flash drinking so much, she knew she would soon be broke.

Kathy could get an advance from Hank, but she didn't want to. She wanted him to know that she could take care of Flash without help from adults. And she wanted him to know that she was old enough to have a horse of her own.

Maybe she should borrow from Jay even if she had to pay interest. She wouldn't dare offer to buy a foal with no money down. Mr. Richfield might laugh at her.

"Sure," Jay said when Kathy asked for a loan. "I'll lend you four dollars at ten percent."

"That should be enough for today and tomorrow," Kathy said. "You keep track of the bill. I'll pay you when I get my allowance."

Jay scribbled a note on a slip of paper and stuffed it in his pocket. Then he helped Kathy lug the milk home from the store. Today Flo let them store it in the refrigerator. And she helped mix the egg white in it. Sometimes Flo was all right, Kathy thought.

After lunch Kathy heated some of the formula. "You can help me give Flash this bottle," she said to Jay as they walked toward the stables.

"No thanks." Jay twitched his nose. "I don't want any part of this horse business. Did I ever tell you about the five St. Bernards I used to own when I lived in New York?"

"You told me," Kathy said. *And I didn't believe a word of it,* she added in her thoughts.

Jay took his usual place by the corral fence as Kathy headed for Flash's stall. When the foal saw Kathy coming, she trotted to meet her. But somehow she couldn't stop when she reached Kathy. Kathy tried to sidestep, but she was too late.

Flash knocked her off balance. As she hit the ground, Kathy tasted gritty dust and felt some of the warm milk dribble down her arm. Hank shouted and hobbled toward them, but Kathy needed no help. She was already back on her feet.

81

"You all right?" Hank asked, his eyes clouded with concern.

"Sure." Kathy forced a smile. She knew they were both remembering Dr. Pillum's words about feeding Flash being a man's job. "Flash didn't mean to knock me down. She's still wobbly on her legs. She couldn't help it. I won't let it happen again, Hank."

Once he was sure Kathy wasn't hurt, Hank gave her a long look. She felt as if he could read her very thoughts. But he said nothing.

Now that Flash was feeling better, she was more playful. Sometimes she sucked on the nipple and swallowed great gulps of milk. Other times she just snapped the nipple with her teeth. This trick sent milk spraying all over everything, but mostly all over Kathy's clothes. Still, most of the milk ended up inside the foal.

Jay had gone home, and it was almost suppertime when the accident happened. Afterwards, Kathy couldn't quite remember what had caused it. But she was willing to take the blame. Flash was a gentle foal. She wouldn't have bitten anyone on purpose.

She must have had her thumb too close to the nipple.

"What happened?" Hank called as Kathy dropped Flash's bottle, sucked on her injured thumb, and started to dance a jig in the corral.

"N-nothing." She fought back tears.

"Let's see that thumb." Hank limped toward her and took her hand.

"It doesn't hurt," Kathy lied. "It's just a s-scratch."

"I know what a horse bite feels like," Hank said, his voice gruff. "Feels like the very devil's clamped his teeth into you. Now you scat for home and wash this thumb. Dose it with medicine, then get yourself to the doctor.

"The d-doctor?" Kathy's voice quavered. "But it's hardly bleeding."

"The doctor," Hank insisted. "You need a tetanus shot. No worse place in all the world for tetanus germs than around horses. But a shot'll fix you up. You hear me?"

"Y-yes," Kathy said. "I'll tell Dad."

"And if he's not home, you tell Flo." Kathy nodded. When she reached the house she found Flo and Jay there alone. Before she could say a word, Flo yelled, "Kathy! That smell! What on earth!"

"It's just milk, Flo. Flash is sort of a messy eater, and . . ."

"And you come home smelling like a cheese factory! Get out of those clothes. No—not here. Go to the basement and skin out of them down there. And leave them by the washing machine."

Kathy got her robe and ran for the basement, tears blurring her sight. Where was her dad? Why wasn't he ever around when she needed him?

By the time Kathy showered and changed clothes, Mr. Duncan had arrived. Flo told him about the clothes and the sour smell. His mouth was a straight line across his face. Kathy kept her throbbing thumb in her lap all during supper. He didn't notice, but Jay did.

"What's wrong with your hand?" Jay asked in a voice pitched to win everyone's attention.

Kathy ignored him, but he repeated the question even louder.

"What's the trouble, Kathy?" her dad asked. "Let's see your hand."

Kathy held up her unhurt hand. "Nothing's wrong, Dad." She held up her other hand, but she kept her thumb tucked out of sight.

"Kathy, go wash again," he said. "Part of the corral's under those fingernails."

Kathy scowled at Jay, but she welcomed her escape from the table. She couldn't tell her dad about her thumb now—not in front of Jay and Flo. That Jay! Why couldn't he keep his mouth shut?

At bedtime Kathy's stomach felt as if she had been riding a spinning merry-go-round. She wondered what happened to people who caught tetanus. Was it as bad as measles? Or whooping cough? Maybe it was worse. Maybe she would die from it. Then Jay would be sorry for being a stinker.

Kathy tried to sleep, but her whole hand ached. She could feel her pulse pounding under her thumbnail. Suddenly she jumped from bed. She didn't want to die—not even to get away from Jay. But what if she was too late? The doctor's office had closed long ago.

Chapter Thirteen
A Tetanus Shot

Kathy snapped on her bedside lamp. It was midnight. She wanted her dad to wake up, but her throat ached and she was afraid to call to him. Slipping into her robe, she crept into the bathroom. She splashed lots of water into the sink. No one heard. She flushed the toilet three times.

"Are you sick, Kathy?" Mr. Duncan towered in the bathroom doorway, yawning and rubbing his eyes.

Kathy didn't know she was crying until she felt the hot, wet tears rolling down her cheeks. She held up her throbbing thumb.

"Hank told me to get a tetanus shot," she said, "but I was afraid to tell anyone. Flo was already mad at me about the sour milk smell."

"What happened, Kathy?" her dad examined the thumb.

"Flash bit me. She didn't mean to. She really loves me, but I got my thumb in her way. And now it's too l-late. What's tetanus like, Dad?"

Mr. Duncan put an arm around Kathy's shoulders until her sobs quieted. "Tetanus is a deadly sickness, but you're not going to have it. I'll get you an aspirin to stop the pain, and then I'll drive you to the doctor in the morning." He took the aspirin bottle from the medicine chest and filled a glass with water.

"W-won't morning be too l-late?" Kathy asked after swallowing the aspirin.

"No. If you have a booster shot within a day after an injury, you'll be safe. You still have plenty of time. But why didn't you tell me about this at dinner?"

"I was afraid."

"You've never been afraid of needles before," he said.

Kathy stared at her toes. She couldn't tell her dad the whole truth. She couldn't tell him that she had been afraid of what he would say. But he didn't pry. As he tucked her back into bed, it was almost like old times. Old times before Jay. Kathy offered her dad one of the crackers she kept hidden under her pillow. She smiled when he took it, and she felt better as she ate one too. He said nothing while they ate but tousled her hair before he turned out the light and left her.

The next morning Jay fairly bristled with advice.

"It won't hurt if you don't watch the needle. If you sort of stiffen up your arm, you'll only feel a prick." He wrinkled his forehead and demonstrated the correct arm position.

"I've had lots and lots of shots," Jay said. "Why, once I had five shots at the same time. There was tetanus, whooping cough, measles, mumps, and . . . and . . . Gee, I can't remember the other one. But there were five. I didn't even flinch. The doctor made a big thing of it. He called in several nurses and two other doctors. He even said he might send an article about me to one of the medical magazines."

Horsefeathers! Horsefeathers! Kathy stopped listening as Jay continued bragging. As soon as Flo was out of the kitchen, she heated two bottles of formula for Flash.

Mr. Duncan came into the kitchen and said, "I'll drive you to the doctor's office on my way to work."

"Okay," Kathy answered. She hated to ask Jay to go with her to the stables, but she wanted to please her dad.

"Want to come along, Jay? I'll let you hold one bottle."

"No thanks," Jay said. "I've got to eat breakfast."

The sweet scent of the bluestem grass filled the morning air, and Kathy breathed deeply. She liked the heat of the blazing sun on her head and shoulders. Now that last night's terrible fear was gone, she almost bounced as she walked.

At the stables Flash trotted to meet Kathy, and she was careful not to let the foal knock her down again. Flash didn't play with the rubber nipple this morning. She was hungry. She drained both bottles, hardly pausing for breath.

"She's doing fine," Hank said, limping over to pat Flash's head. "You've saved her life, Kathy. Don't think I won't tell Mr. Richfield what you've done for him."

"I really did it for Flash," Kathy said. "Hank, would you hint to Mr. Richfield that I'd like to buy Flash?"

"No point in thinking that way and getting your hopes all up," Hank said. "Mr. Richfield's not apt to part with this foal. Course, I'm sure he'll have some kind of a reward for you."

"I don't want any reward. I want Flash."

"You'll just make yourself miserable wanting something you can't have. Did you get that tetanus shot?"

"Dad's taking me to the doctor this morning."

"Then you scoot for home," Hank ordered. "Don't show up back here until you've had it."

Kathy knew her dad wouldn't be ready to go to town so early, so she took time to groom Flash. She began with the dandy brush, working from head to tail. Flash liked to be brushed, and she stood still better than she had when her mother was alive. Kathy worked on her mane with the currycomb until it fell against her tan hide like silk fringe.

It was time to begin working with Flash's feet. Mr. Richfield had said the sooner the better. Kathy hesitated for a moment trying to remember all that Hank had taught her about grooming horses' hooves. Standing carefully at Flash's near side, she ran her right hand gently down one leg clear to the hoof. Flash stood still as the corral gate. Kathy repeated this twice, and then she gently tried to lift the hoof.

At first she couldn't budge it. But as she pushed her shoulder against Flash's side, the foal shifted her balance. She let Kathy lift the hoof, clean it with a hoof pick, and place it back on the ground. Kathy could hardly believe her success. She repeated the process on Flash's right hoof before she turned the foal loose and started for home. The rear feet could wait until another day.

When she got home, Kathy was bursting to tell someone of her success. Her dad and Flo were talking over their coffee. Jay was the only one available, so she swallowed her words. He wouldn't understand. And he would try to top her story.

Kathy grinned. Five seemed to be Jay's special number. She wondered if he had ever groomed a foal with five feet.

Kathy felt important riding to town with her father. She hardly ever got to be alone with him anymore. But now that they were together, she could think of nothing to say.

Her dad went inside the medical clinic with her. The whole building smelled like a big bottle of medicine. Nurses and receptionists rushed about in their flat-heeled shoes, white uniforms, and caps. Kathy didn't even see the doctor. The nurse just talked to him, then gave Kathy the shot.

She hardly felt the needle. Kathy grinned at her dad and he winked at her. Too bad Jay wasn't there to see how brave she was. She thought about making up a whopping story to tell him, but she decided against it. She knew she couldn't beat Jay at his own game. She would play it cool. If he learned anything about her visit to the doctor, he would have to pry it from her.

Once outside the clinic Kathy told her dad good-bye. She wanted to run all the way home. But it was too far. And it was too hot. She walked a block, then she ran a block. Dr. Pillum saw her and gave her a ride for six blocks. His car tires made a squishing sound in the hot tar on the street. It was ten o'clock when she walked through her own front doorway—time for Flash's next feeding.

"Was it bad?" Jay asked.

"Of course not," Kathy said. "You should know that."

Kathy put two more bottles of formula on to heat while she changed clothes. When the milk was warm, she headed for the stables without inviting Jay. But he tagged along, his secret sketchbook under his arm.

At the corral Kathy had trouble opening the blue gate. Someone had looped the chain backward; she had to set the milk bottles down to straighten it out. Jay caught up with her, but he didn't offer to help.

Kathy finally got the chain straightened, and swung the gate open. Jay stepped inside the corral and Kathy stooped to pick up the milk bottles. He didn't, of course, think to close the gate. She had to set the bottles down again and do it herself.

She had no more than picked the bottles back up when she saw Flash cantering toward them.

"Watch out, Jay!" Kathy yelled.

Jay's sketchbook flew into the air as he scrambled over the corral gate and ran toward home.

Chapter Fourteen
The Secret of the
Secret Sketchbook

Jay's secret was out. Pictures from his sketchbook fluttered like leaves in the light breeze. Kathy grabbed the bottles of formula and carried them to the safety of the tack shed. Returning to the corral, she scurried after Jay's sketches with Flash trotting playfully at her heels. In spite of all she could do, the foal stepped on several of the pictures, grinding them into the dust.

All the sketches were of horses. And they were good. She recognized Dynamite and Blitzen and Flash. She stared, puzzled. Jay hated horses. Or did he? How could anyone hate horses, yet draw such beautiful pictures of them? She stacked the sketches in a neat pile. There wasn't one picture of a St. Bernard, or any other kind of dog. And dogs were Jay's favorite animal. Slipping the

sketches back in the sketchbook, Kathy carried it into the tack shed where it would be safe.

"Need some help with the foal?" Hank asked, hobbling through the back door of the shed.

"No thanks," Kathy said. "Everything's fine. Jay just dropped his sketchbook, and I brought it in here for the time being."

"Can't imagine him turning loose of that book." Hank tapped his pipe against his wooden leg. "What happened?"

"Flash startled him. She ran toward us when we brought her milk. Guess Jay thought she was chasing us."

"I'm not surprised," Hank said. "Not surprised at all."

Kathy wished she hadn't said so much. That Jay! Why did he have to run like a scared rabbit? What if Hank got it into his head that Flash was dangerous? Kathy slipped from the tack shed with the foal's breakfast. She fed her and rinsed out the bottles.

Attaching a lead rope to Flash's halter, Kathy tied her to a hitching rail. Flash sniffed the dandy brush and currycomb and rolled her eyes, but she stood still while Kathy groomed her once again.

Kathy's brush strokes grew hard and fast as she thought about Jay's behavior. He couldn't fool her. He was trying to get her in trouble again. This time with Hank. He was trying to make it look as if Flash were dangerous. He was trying to make Kathy lose her job.

As soon as she turned Flash loose, Kathy got Jay's sketchbook. She headed for home with anger churning deep inside. Once in the house she counted to ten, then she found Jay and handed him his pictures.

"I caught them before they blew away."

"You snooped." Jay grabbed his book and clutched it like a shield in front of his chest. "Those pictures were supposed to be top secret."

"I didn't have to pick them up for you," Kathy said. "I could have let them blow away. Why'd you run off like that?" She glared at Jay until he squirmed.

"I thought Flash was going to trample me." Jay's voice was so low and his face so flushed that Kathy knew she had been wrong. He was telling the truth. And the truth embarrassed him.

"You're a good artist," she said, trying to change the subject, trying to sort out her thoughts about Jay. "Those pictures are great. But I thought you hated horses."

For a long time Jay just stood there clutching his sketchbook and wrinkling his forehead. Then he sighed.

"I think horses are great—from a distance. They're so big . . ."

Suddenly Kathy understood. Jay had been afraid of Flash. He hadn't been trying to get her in trouble with Hank. He was afraid of horses. Jay was . . . afraid.

For a moment Kathy could think of nothing to say. Day before yesterday she might have laughed. But now she knew what real fear was like. She remembered how she had felt only the night before when she had thought she was going to die from tetanus.

Fear was no laughing matter. It could make a person do crazy things like flushing the toilet three times in the middle of the

99

night. Or like crying over a sore thumb. It might even make a person brag.

All at once she understood Jay. The events of the past days rolled across her mind like a TV film. Jay had faced a Kansas thunderhead in order to avoid riding Dynamite. He hadn't been trying to get her in trouble with her dad. He had refused to help feed Flash because he had been afraid. His busyness with his sketchbook was just a cover-up to hide his fear.

Kathy empathized with Jay. Empathize. That was a big word that she liked. It meant she understood how Jay felt. It was hard to dislike someone you understood.

For the first time Kathy forgot herself and her troubles. For the first time she thought about how Jay must feel. He had said that he hated Kansas. And no wonder. All his friends were in New York. And she had done nothing to help him make new friends here. In fact, she hadn't even seen her own friends since Flo made a bathroom out of the backyard.

"Horses are big," Kathy said, not knowing yet how to put her new thoughts into words. "But they don't know it. That's your secret. If you pretend that you're just as big as they are, they'll believe you. When we go back to the stables, I'll help you make friends with Dynamite."

Kathy's offer didn't relieve Jay's fear. When she returned to the stables for Flash's next feeding, Jay stayed at home. As she opened the corral gate, Hank limped toward her. His silver-framed glasses had slid down on his nose, and he paused to push them back.

"I've fixed up a new feeding station," he said. "Shouldn't have waited this long to do it."

"What do you mean?" Kathy was afraid that Hank might not need her to feed Flash.

Hank motioned for her to follow him. "There're some big problems in bottle feeding a foal," he said. "One problem is that the foal may get so it almost knocks you down trying to reach the milk. When a foal's little, people think that's a cute trick. But as it gets older, the 'trick' becomes downright dangerous."

"But what can we do about it?" Kathy

asked, accenting the word *we*. "Flash can't eat without these bottles."

"Come back here." Hank led the way through a passage behind Flash's stall. "I've built a rack back here to hold the bottle. See?" He took a bottle from Kathy, placed it in the rack, and pushed it through a round hole into Flash's stall.

"The hole's small enough that Flash can't pull the bottle clear inside the stall. Yet it's tilted so she can suck out the last drop of milk. From now on you can come in through the barn and put the milk in place before she ever sees you."

Kathy and Hank walked around to Flash's stall and showed the foal the new source of food. Once she saw it, she ate as eagerly as if Kathy were holding the bottle. As they were watching, Dr. Pillum arrived to give her another vitamin shot.

"Called my son in Emporia last night," he said in his no-hurry way. "He's willing for my grandson to have this foal when she's weaned if Mr. Richfield will sell." Dr. Pillum patted Flash's coat with a pudgy hand. "I'll offer a good price for this one.

Look at the shape of her head. I can always spot good breeding in the head shape."

"Don't think making an offer will do you a speck of good," Hank muttered. The two of them discussed the topic for several minutes. When Dr. Pillum left, Kathy was near tears.

"Hank, you can't let Mr. Richfield sell Flash to Dr. Pillum. You just can't."

"Kathy, now see here," Hank said. "I have no say about what Mr. Richfield does. You know that."

"I know. But you could speak up for me, couldn't you? You could tell him that Flash loves me."

"I'll not be saying any lies for you or anyone else," Hank said.

"It's no lie," Kathy argued. "Flash loves me. You know she does."

"I know nothing of the sort. You've been reading too many books."

"But she comes running every time she sees me. She does! She does!"

"Sure," Hank said. "But that doesn't prove love. What horses do, they do from habit. Or from the memory of often-repeated signals. Their 'love' is of the cupboard variety. Any tame creature associates humans with food. Flash loves food, not you."

Kathy felt tears sliding down her cheeks, but she couldn't stop them.

"Now, don't you go a-watering my corral with your tears. You're expecting more from Flash than any critter can offer. You might as well face the truth. Don't expect too much. Don't ask more than Flash can give. If you treat this foal with kindness and firmness, she'll be willing and eager to please you. But love? Never!"

Chapter Fifteen
Mr. Richfield Returns

Kathy kicked a flat stone all the way from the corral to her back door. Hank was wrong. Hank was wise in the ways of horses. But this time he was wrong. Hadn't she saved Flash's life? Hadn't she nursed Flash back to health when everyone else expected her to die? It didn't seem fair for someone else to own her.

Kathy beelined to her room, banged the door shut, and flopped across her bed. Nibbling a cracker, she tried to think only of the salty taste in her mouth. But her mind was spinning. What would happen tomorrow when Mr. Richfield came home? Would he sell Flash to Dr. Pillum? Kathy thought she couldn't stand it if Flash were taken from her.

On the following morning Kathy had

given Flash her first feeding when Jay appeared at the corral.

"Did you mean it when you said you'd teach me to ride?" He wrinkled his forehead, twitched his nose, and chewed his gum all at the same time.

Kathy had been so upset over the possibility that Flash would be sold that she had forgotten all about Jay.

"I never said I'd teach you to ride," she replied, surprised that Jay had nerve enough to ask. "I said I'd help you make friends with the horses. There're a lot of things to learn before you start riding."

"Huh!" Jay exclaimed. "You just think I can't stick in the saddle. Why, once I rode for five hours without stopping." His voice faded away, and Kathy saw a red flush spread from his neck to his hairline.

"I was just kidding, Kathy. Really, I was. I've never been on a horse in all my life."

Kathy grinned. Maybe Jay wasn't so bad after all. "Lots of people have never ridden a horse," she said. "And they're missing out on a lot of fun."

Kathy let Jay come with her to Dynamite's

stall. He watched while she put halter and lead rope on the chestnut mare and led her into the corral.

"Now, you hold the lead rope while I curry her," Kathy said.

Jay held the rope by the very tip end, standing as far from Dynamite as he could.

"She won't bite, will she?"

Kathy shook her head. "While you're standing there, pat her head and talk to her. That'll make her feel at ease with you. I'll let you help exercise her later."

Jay eased toward Dynamite and touched her head as if it were a hot stove. Nothing happened. She just pricked her ears forward. As soon as Jay discovered that Dynamite was gentle, he patted her with more ease.

"Her nose feels like Mom's velvet dress," Jay said.

At that announcement, Dynamite snorted, and Jay almost fell in his haste to back away.

"She just sneezed," Kathy said. "You must have tickled her nose, but she won't hurt you. You'll make her jittery if you act

107

afraid. Horses can sense when people are afraid of them."

Kathy finished her comb and brush job before she led Dynamite to the riding ring next to the corral. She gave Jay the lead rope. Then she showed him how to walk around the ring with the mare, keeping at her side close to her shoulder.

"What if she starts running?" Jay asked.

"She won't run unless something scares her. All the horses at the Bluestem obey spoken commands. If you say 'walk', she'll walk. If you say 'trot', she'll trot. And if you say 'canter,' you better be on her back. You'd never be able to keep up by running at her side."

Kathy walked with Jay as he circled Dynamite once around the ring.

"Okay, you're on your own," she said. "Take her around three more times; then you can walk Blitzen while I saddle Dynamite."

Kathy began currying Blitzen while Jay walked Dynamite around the ring. For a beginner he was doing quite well even though he was still ill at ease and wary.

Kathy hadn't noticed Hank enter the corral. She jumped when he spoke to her.

"Never thought I'd see that lad on the other end of a lead rope," he said, grinning.

"You knew he was afraid of horses?" Kathy asked.

"Yup. He might as well have worn a sign that said so. But he seems to be doing well now."

"I didn't know how he felt about horses until yesterday." Kathy wondered if she would ever be as wise as Hank. "I just thought he hated them."

"That should have been a clue," Hank said. "Most folks dislike whatever they're afraid of."

Kathy wondered. Did she dislike Jay because she was afraid of him? How silly, she thought. She wasn't afraid of Jay King. Not at all. She was taller than he was and at least five pounds heavier. But the back of her mind wasn't so sure. Maybe she was afraid Jay would take her place with her father. Kathy changed the subject.

"Hank, do you know what I dreamed last night?"

"Now, just how would I know that?" he asked, lighting his pipe.

"I dreamed that Mr. Richfield gave Flash to me because I saved her life."

"That's one dream that's not apt to come true," Hank said. "Nobody gives a foal away—unless its mother is a rodeo horse."

"What difference does that make?" Kathy asked, sorry that she had told Hank about her dream.

"Performing in rodeos is hard work. A foal takes a mare's mind off her business in the arena. A rodeo rider might give a foal away, but not a ranch owner like Mr. Richfield."

Kathy wished she could stop thinking of Flash as her foal. She sighed and led Blitzen to the ring where Jay was still walking Dynamite.

"She likes me!" Jay said, smiling. "She's just walking along gentle as can be."

"That's because she's a well-trained horse." Kathy's words slipped out automatically. Then she remembered Hank's reply when she had told him that Flash loved her. "And because she likes you," she added.

Kathy scowled. She saddled Dynamite and trotted her around the ring while Jay led Blitzen.

Kathy heard tires crunch against gravel. Looking up, she saw a black station wagon coming up the ranch driveway. It was Mr. Richfield in a dark business suit, white shirt, and tie. As he climbed from his car, Kathy noticed his wide-set eyes, eyes that always smiled at children and horses.

"It's Mr. Richfield." Kathy dropped her voice to a whisper. "Come on, Jay. Take Blitzen's lead rope off and turn her into the pasture. I'll unsaddle Dynamite. I want to hear everything Mr. Richfield has to say."

Chapter Sixteen
The Accident

"Can't you just turn her loose with the saddle on for a few minutes?" Jay asked.

Kathy shook her head. "She might roll on the ground and break it. Jay . . ." Kathy hesitated, hating to ask favors of her step-brother. "Would you do something for me?"

"What?" he asked.

"Go home and heat two more bottles of formula," Kathy said. "I'd do it, but I don't want to miss out on anything Mr. Richfield says to Hank."

"Okay," said Jay. "On one condition."

"What's that?" Kathy asked, irritated at the delay.

"On the condition that you'll teach me to ride."

Kathy sighed. "When you're ready, I'll teach you."

Jay headed for home. Kathy had Dynamite's saddle and bridle back in the tack shed by the time Mr. Richfield had greeted Hank and heard all the stable news.

The day had grown hot and still. The prairie breeze had died down, and the sun turned the corral into a forge. Kathy felt heat rising from the ground in suffocating vapors. She eased beside Hank as the men peered into Flash's stall. The wood was hot to the touch, and Kathy kept her hands in her pockets. When Mr. Richfield noticed her, he spoke. His voice was as friendly as his eyes.

"Hank tells me that you saved Flash's life, Kathy. Anything to that story?"

Kathy felt her face flush. "Flash was bad off when I found her. We've been feeding her from a bottle."

"You've done a great job," Mr. Richfield said. "I'm sure Flash wouldn't be here today if it hadn't been for you. I must owe you quite a bit of money for all the milk you've been buying. Do you know how much?"

Kathy shook her head. She couldn't take money for anything she had done for Flash.

But before she could tell him how she felt, Hank spoke up.

"Kathy wouldn't let me pay the bill. She borrowed most of the milk money from her stepbrother. Jay gave me a list of the amounts. Got it right here in my pocket."

"But . . ." Kathy scowled and kicked at the dust.

"Now don't go gittin' riled," Hank said. "You need a little business sense along with all that horse sense. I guessed you'd never give anyone a bill, so I made Jay hand it over."

Kathy wished that the ground would open up and swallow her. That Jay! Just when she had decided he might be all right, he had to double-cross her like this. Hadn't she promised him he'd get his money back? And with interest! What would Mr. Richfield think?

Mr. Richfield studied the creased sheet of paper Hank gave him for several moments. Then he reached into his inside coat pocket and pulled out his checkbook and pen.

"There you are, Kathy." He pressed the check into her unwilling hand. "Pay your

114

debt to Jay and keep the extra for yourself as a token of my thanks."

"Mr. Richfield," Kathy blurted, not even looking at the check. "What are you going to do with Flash?"

He paused so long that Kathy spoke again. "What I mean is, I'd like to go on taking care of her. What I *really* mean is, I'd like to buy her. I haven't much money, but I could pay you a few dollars down. I'd work forever to earn the rest of it."

Mr. Richfield pulled a letter from his pocket. "Here's a note from Dr. Pillum offering me five hundred dollars for the foal. What's going on here anyway? Why does everyone think I want to sell?"

"I didn't think you'd want to be bothered with bottle-feeding a foal," Kathy said.

"But you're bottle-feeding Flash for me, aren't you?" Mr. Richfield asked. "You're not planning to quit, are you?"

"Oh, no sir," Kathy said, proud that Mr. Richfield thought she could manage Flash.

Just then Jay stepped into the corral carrying the two bottles of warm formula. Before Kathy or Hank could shout a warning, Flash galloped toward him. Jay froze. Kathy saw the terror in his eyes.

Everything happened so fast Kathy could only stand and stare. Flash knocked Jay down. Before he could roll out of the way, her sharp hooves cut into his leg and into his left hand.

Jay let out one shrill shriek. His face turned as white as the formula in the bottles he had dropped. He lay motionless in the hot dust.

Chapter Seventeen
Custody—and a Partnership

At last Kathy sprang into action. Grabbing a bottle of milk, she coaxed Flash away from Jay.

"Hank! Hank!" Kathy cried. "Do something."

It was Mr. Richfield who responded. He sprinted toward the telephone in the tack shed. Hank bent over Jay's quiet form, shading him from the blazing sun. It seemed that hours passed before Flo came streaking toward the corral, her yellow hair streaming over her shoulders. Kathy ran to open the gate.

"Where is he?" Flo looked directly at Kathy. "Why isn't someone doing something for him? Where's a phone? I must call Rick."

"I've called your husband as well as the

doctor, ma'am," Mr. Richfield said, stepping from the tack shed. "It's best not to
move an injured person. Might cause worse
trouble."

"How did this happen?" With no thought
for her pink silk slacks, Flo knelt in the dust
at Jay's side.

"The foal . . ." Kathy began, but Flo
interrupted her.

"Get that wild beast away from here!" She
moved so her body was between Jay and
Flash. "That brute's a menace. I'll see that
it's disposed of. I'll . . ."

"It wasn't Flash's fault," Kathy said. "It
was . . . my fault. I forgot to tell Jay about
the new feeding rack behind Flash's stall.
She saw Jay with her milk. She just got so
eager that she accidentally knocked him
down. Flash didn't mean any harm, Flo.
Honest, she didn't."

Hank had brought a bucket of water and a
cloth, and Flo began bathing Jay's forehead.
Kathy wondered why Flo didn't bathe his
leg and his hand, which were bleeding. She
decided that the best thing she could do was
to feed Flash and keep her out of the way.

Again Kathy fought tears. It scared her to see Jay sprawled there in the dust. And Flo's threats frightened her. She felt alone. And the heat was unbearable. Surely there was another thunderhead on the way.

Flash had emptied both milk bottles when Dr. Bently arrived. He was a tall, thin man with slightly stooped shoulders. He moved with a calmness that was reassuring.

Flo was almost hysterical. Kathy couldn't speak, but Hank and Mr. Richfield explained the situation to the doctor.

All Kathy could do was stare at Jay. She had never seen anyone lie so still and look so white before. She couldn't bear to watch as Dr. Bently ran his hands over Jay's body, then searched in his black bag for antiseptic and bandages.

"Let's move him to the shade," he said.

Mr. Richfield helped Dr. Bently carry Jay to a cot in the tack shed. Kathy felt only slight relief when her father sprinted toward them from the lane where he had left his car. Jay's eyes were still closed, and Dr. Bently was applying bandages.

"Rick!" Flo shouted and jumped up when

her husband entered the tack shed. "Jay and Kathy are never to come near these stables again." She clutched Rick's arm. "Never! Never!"

Before Kathy's father could answer, Jay opened his eyes. His face was still paper white. He looked up into the doctor's face.

"You fainted, son," Dr. Bently said. "But you'll be all right. No concussion. No broken bones. You'll have to come to my office for a day or two to have these cuts dressed, but you'll be good as new in a few days."

The Duncans and Mr. Richfield thanked the doctor. As soon as Jay sat up on the edge of the cot, Dr. Bently hurried on his way. Kathy thought relief was one of the nicest feelings on earth. She was surprised to find she had actually been worried about Jay.

"Jay!" Flo cried and hugged her son. "You're never to go near those horses again. Never! And neither is Kathy."

"Don't say that, Flo," Mr. Duncan said, slipping an arm around Kathy's waist. "A person ought to face the thing that frightens him."

"You don't want to go near the horses do you, Jay?" Flo asked.

Jay said nothing for several moments. When he spoke, his voice was shaky, but even Kathy was surprised at his words. She looked at him with new respect.

"Kathy's going to teach me to ride," he said. "Just as soon as I'm better."

Rick smiled at Flo until Flo smiled in spite of herself.

"That-a-boy, Jay," Mr. Richfield said, grinning. "You're welcome at the Bluestem any time."

"I'll let Jay work with the gentle mares," said Kathy. "And you won't need to worry about Flash, Flo." Her voice dropped to a whisper. "I think Dr. Pillum is going to buy her and take her away."

"You're thinking wrong," Mr. Richfield said, patting Jay on the shoulder. "Don't you want to take care of Flash, Kathy?"

"Of course I do. You know I do. But Dr. Pillum . . . five hundred dollars . . ."

"No amount of money will buy Flash," Mr. Richfield said. "And I hereby give you custody of that foal. She's still mine, but you're to feed her and work with her as long as she needs it."

Before Kathy could speak, Mr. Richfield turned to Jay. "And you seem to have a brain for business, young man. I'll give you custody of enough money to buy whatever milk, eggs, and syrup are needed. Is that a deal?"

Kathy and Jay nodded, and Mr. Richfield shook hands with them to seal the bargain. When Jay felt better the Duncans told Mr. Richfield good-bye and went home.

At the house Kathy's father followed her to her room. After settling Jay in an easy chair, Flo went to pour them all a cool drink.

"So you have custody of a foal," Mr. Duncan said, smiling. "Having custody is an honor as well as a great responsibility."

"Do you really think so?" Kathy asked.

"Of course," her father replied. "You shouldn't undertake it unless you love Flash very much."

Kathy couldn't begin to tell her dad her feelings for Flash or for him. She wondered why people had so much trouble saying important things to each other.

"Jay has custody of the milk money," Kathy said, smiling. "Guess he and I are partners."

For the first time in weeks Kathy saw her dad smile the old smile she had been wanting to see for so long—the smile that was especially for her.

That night Kathy stood at her open window and stared out across the vast moonlit prairie. The breeze had returned, and the stifling heat was gone. The threat of a thunderhead had vanished. Custody. Custody. The word kept singing through Kathy's mind.

Custody—she loved that word. And she loved Flash. And she felt that Flash loved her.

Kathy left the window open so she could smell the sweet fragrance of the bluestem grass as she lay in bed thinking. She still didn't have a horse of her own, but she had custody. And she had a partnership that was almost sure to lead to a friendship. She drifted to sleep with dreams of Flash, her family, and the bluestem prairie.

Glossary of Terms

canter—an easy gallop or run

curry—to rub and clean a horse with a currycomb

currycomb—a comb with rows of metal teeth for currying horses

dandy brush—a brush with stiff short bristles that is used for grooming horses

dun—a grayish brown color

forge—a fireplace hearth for heating metal

gait—a manner of walking, stepping, running; a way of going

gallop—to run rapidly; to ride at full speed

gulley—a small valley or ditch worn away by running water

halter—a rope or strap with a headpiece for leading horses

halter class—a division in a horse show in which the horse is led around the show ring wearing only a halter

hoof pick—a sharp metal tool for cleaning a horse's hooves

near side—left side

ominous—threatening

polychrome—a picture in many colors

quarter horse—a breed of strong horses developed for short-distance races, usually a quarter of a mile

trot—a gait between a walk and a run

wary—on guard

withers—the highest part of the horse's back, at the base of the neck